Karen's Ski Trip

**Look for these
and other books about Karen
in the
Baby-sitters Little Sister series:**

Little Sister

Karen's Ski Trip

Ann M. Martin

Illustrations by Susan Tang

A
LITTLE APPLE
PAPERBACK

SCHOLASTIC INC.
New York Toronto London Auckland Sydney

ISBN 0-590-48304-8

Copyright © 1995 by Ann M. Martin.
All rights reserved. Published by Scholastic Inc.
BABY-SITTERS LITTLE SISTER ® and APPLE PAPERBACKS ® are registered trademarks of Scholastic Inc.

12 11 10 9 8 7 6 5 4 3 2 1   5 6 7 8 9/9 0/0

Printed in the U.S.A.   40

First Scholastic printing, February 1995

*The author gratefully acknowledges
Stephanie Calmenson
for her help
with this book.*

Karen's Ski Trip

1

Exciting News

"Hello, Moosie. How have you been?" I asked. I gave Moosie a big hug.

Moosie is my stuffed cat. He lives at the big house where my daddy lives. I had not seen him in one whole month.

"Goosie asked me to say hello to you," I said.

Goosie is my other stuffed cat. He lives at the little house where my mommy lives.

That is right. I have two houses. I will

tell you more about them later. But first I will tell you about me.

My name is Karen Brewer. I am seven years old. I have blonde hair, blue eyes, and a bunch of freckles. I wear glasses, too. I have two pairs. I have a blue pair for reading. I have a pink pair to wear the rest of the time. (I do not wear any glasses at all when I am in the bath or sleeping.)

Knock, knock. Elizabeth was standing outside my room. Elizabeth is my stepmother.

"It is almost time for dinner," she said. "Nannie is cooking."

"I will be right there," I replied.

I quickly put away my things. Then I washed up and went downstairs.

Sniff, sniff. I wiggled my nose in the air like a puppy. *Sniff, sniff.*

"Something smells good," I said.

"I made one of your favorite dinners," said Nannie. "It is lasagna."

Yum! I love lasagna. Especially Nannie's. (Nannie is Elizabeth's mother. That makes her my stepgrandmother.)

"Would you like to help set the table?" asked Elizabeth.

"Sure," I replied.

I did a gigundoly good job. I put everything where it belonged. I even remembered the napkins.

In no time my whole big-house family was sitting at the table. There are ten of us, including Andrew and me. Andrew is my little brother. He is four going on five. Then there are the grown-ups. They are Daddy, Elizabeth, and Nannie. The rest are my stepsister, stepbrothers, and adopted sister. There is Kristy, who is thirteen and the best stepsister ever; David Michael who is seven; Sam and Charlie, who are so old they are in high school; and Emily Michelle, my adopted sister, who is two and a half.

We had a lot to catch up on. We had a

lot we had to eat, too. Lasagna, salad, green beans, and bread.

Clink, clink, clink!

"Attention, everyone," said Daddy. "I have something to tell you."

I could tell it was going to be something important. I sat up tall in my chair.

"Today is the first day of February," said Daddy. "That means winter break is just a week away. Elizabeth and I have planned a special trip for the family."

"Yes!" I cried.

"Where are we going?" asked Sam.

"We are going up to Shadow Lake," said Elizabeth.

"I love Shadow Lake!" I said.

Shadow Lake is in western Massachusetts. Daddy has a cabin up there. Really it is more than a cabin. It is a house. We have been there in the summer. But we never have been there in the winter.

"Mitch has just finished winterizing the house for us," said Daddy. (Mitch is the caretaker.) "So now we can use it in cold weather, too."

"There will be lots for us to do," said Elizabeth. "The lodge will be open. You can go skiing and do all kinds of winter sports."

I had been at the big house only a few hours. Already there was exciting news!

2

My Two Houses

I promised to tell you about my two houses. So here is the story.

When I was little I lived in a big house in Stoneybrook, Connecticut. I lived there with Mommy, Daddy, and Andrew. Then Mommy and Daddy started to fight. Soon they were fighting more and more. They tried very hard to get along. But they just could not do it.

Mommy and Daddy explained to Andrew and me that they loved us very much.

But they did not love each other anymore. So they got divorced.

After the divorce, Mommy moved with Andrew and me to a little house not too far away. Then she met a nice man named Seth. Seth and Mommy got married. Now Seth is my stepfather.

Daddy stayed in the big house after the divorce. (It is the house he grew up in.) He met a nice woman named Elizabeth. Elizabeth and Daddy got married. That is how Elizabeth became my stepmother.

So one month Andrew and I live at the little house. The next month we live at the big house. Every month we switch houses.

At the little house are me, Andrew, Mommy, Seth, Rocky (Seth's cat), Midgie (Seth's dog), Emily Junior (my pet rat), and Bob (Andrew's hermit crab).

You already know the people at the big house. They are me, Andrew, Daddy, Elizabeth, Elizabeth's children from her first marriage — Kristy, David Michael, Sam, and Charlie — Nannie, and Emily Michelle. (Emily Michelle was adopted from a faraway country called Vietnam.)

There are pets at the big house, too. They are Shannon (David Michael's puppy), Boo-Boo (Daddy's cat), Crystal Light the Second (my goldfish), Goldfishie (Andrew's you-know-what), Emily Junior, and Bob. (Emily Junior and Bob go back and forth between the two houses with Andrew and me.)

Guess what. I have special nicknames for Andrew and me. I call us Andrew Two-Two and Karen Two-Two. (I got that name from a book my teacher read to our class. The book was called *Jacob Two-Two Meets the Hooded Fang*.) I call us those names because we have two of so many things. That makes going back and forth easier. We have two sets of clothes and books and toys, one at each house. I have my two stuffed cats, Moosie and Goosie. I have two pieces of Tickly, my special blanket. I even have two

8

best friends. Nancy Dawes lives next door to the little house. Hannie Papadakis lives across the street from the big house. (We are in Ms. Colman's second-grade class together. We call ourselves the Three Musketeers.)

Did I leave anything out? I do not think so. Now you know the story of my two houses.

3

Be Careful!

"Have a good vacation, everyone," said Ms. Colman.

It was Friday. It was the last day of school before our winter break.

"You have a good vacation, too!" I said.

I waved good-bye to Ms. Colman. I love my teacher. I was sorry I would not see her for a whole week.

Starting the next day I was not going to see Hannie and Nancy for a whole week either. I was leaving for Shadow Lake first thing in the morning.

The Three Musketeers walked outside together.

Beep beep! Nannie and Emily were waving to us from the Pink Clinker. (That is the name of Nannie's car.)

Instead of riding the school bus, Nannie was driving me, Hannie, and Nancy to the big house. It was going to be a Three Musketeers afternoon.

First Nannie helped us make a very good snack. We had melted cheese on crackers and homemade lemonade. We took our snack upstairs to the playroom. We were going to make-believe we were Lovely Ladies having tea.

"I am in such a tizzy," I said. "There is so much to do before my trip."

"Did you say you were going to the Swiss Alps?" asked Hannie.

"Why, yes," I replied. "I go with my family every winter."

"Have you ever run into Heidi? I hear she lives there," said Nancy.

(Ms. Colman had just read a very won-

11

derful book to our class. It was called *Heidi*. Heidi was a girl who lived in the Alps with her grandfather.)

We finished our snack. Then Hannie and Nancy came into my room to help me pack for my trip.

"Socks. I will need lots of socks," I said. I carried an armful from my drawer and dumped them into my suitcase.

"Sweaters. I will need lots of sweaters," I said. I found four big ones. As soon as they were in my suitcase, there was not much room for anything else.

"You are not going to go skiing, are you?" said Hannie. "I hear it can be pretty dangerous."

"That is true," said Nancy. "A man at my father's office broke his leg. And he was a really good skier."

"He must *not* have been such a good skier. If he was he would not have broken his leg," I replied.

"I do not know about that," said Hannie.

"I hear about a lot of accidents when people go skiing."

"I am not going to have any accidents," I said. "I am very good at ice skating. I am very good at gymnastics. I am sure I will be very good at skiing, too."

"What about Andrew. Is he going to ski?" asked Hannie.

"He says he wants to try," I replied. "Only Andrew is just a little kid. He might have some trouble. But not me. I am going to whiz down the hills."

"I hope you are right," said Hannie.

Ding-dong.

"Nancy, your mom is here to take you home," called Elizabeth.

"I should go, too," said Hannie.

"Have a very good time," said Nancy.

"Thank you. I will," I replied.

We walked downstairs together. Hannie and Nancy were almost out the door when they both turned around. They had worried looks on their faces. At the exact same time they said, "Be careful!"

14

"You do not have to worry about me," I said. I went back to my room to figure out how to get one more sweater into my suitcase.

Hello, House

"**W**ould you like me to help you carry your things downstairs?" asked Daddy.

"No, thank you. I can do it myself," I replied.

I had two bags. I had my knapsack. It was filled with books and crayons and paper. And I had my suitcase. Elizabeth helped me finish packing the night before. It is amazing how much you can fit in when you fold things or roll them up. (I just threw everything inside in a jumble.)

With my knapsack on my back and my

suitcase in my hand, I wobbled out to the driveway.

Andrew tugged at my sleeve. "Karen, will you ride in the van with me?" he asked.

"Sure," I replied. I knew Andrew liked having me with him on long trips. Daddy said our trip to Shadow Lake would take a couple of hours.

My bags were tossed in the back of the van. I sat in the middle. Andrew was on one side of me. David Michael was on the other side. Sam and Charlie sat up front with Daddy. Daddy and Charlie were going to take turns driving.

Elizabeth, Nannie, Kristy, and Emily climbed into the station wagon. (We were leaving our pets behind for the week. Shannon and Boo-Boo were staying at the vet's. Mommy and Seth were taking care of Emily Junior and Bob. And Kristy's friend, Shannon, promised to feed Crystal Light and Goldfishie.)

"Everyone buckle up," said Daddy. "We are on our way!"

We buckled our seat belts. Then Daddy backed out of the driveway and headed for the highway. I waved to all the houses we passed by.

"Good-bye, everyone! Have a nice week," I called.

When we reached the main road, Sam said, "Radio or singing?"

"Singing!" I replied. I began singing "A Hundred Bottles of Pop." I like that song because it takes a really long time. David Michael and Andrew sang it with me.

(Sam, Charlie, and Daddy did not sing. In fact, Charlie was holding his ears most of the time.)

When we finished "A Hundred Bottles of Pop," we sang "The Bear Went Over the Mountain." When we finished "The Bear Went Over the Mountain," we sang "Do Your Ears Hang Low?" We were ready to sing "On Top of Spaghetti" when Andrew announced that he had to go to the bathroom.

18

"No problem," said Daddy. "There is a rest stop up ahead. My ears could use a little rest anyway."

"My throat could use a chocolate shake," I said.

We all got gigundoly delicious refreshments. While we were eating them, the station wagon pulled in. We had a great big party at the rest stop.

"Next stop, Shadow Lake!" said Daddy.

We piled back into our cars. In no time we were pulling into town and heading for the house.

Shadow Lake looked a lot different in the winter than it did in the summer. Now it was all covered with snow. It was very beautiful.

We drove through the town and into the woods. Soon I could see our driveway. Then I saw our house.

"Hello, house!" I called. "We missed you."

I was the first one out of the van and

inside. It felt nice and toasty. There was a pretty bowl of pine cones on the table. A note was taped to the bowl. It said:

Welcome back to Shadow Lake!

Mitch

5

Settling In

"*Knock knock*. Anyone home?" called Mitch.

"Hi, Mitch. Come on in," replied Daddy. "The house looks great. Thank you for getting it ready for us."

"And thank you for these pine cones," I added. "They make excellent moose ears."

I had attached two of them to a wire I had found. I was wearing them on my head. (I promised Andrew I would make a set for him later.)

"I just wanted to make sure you were settling in okay," said Mitch. "You might want to go over to the lodge this afternoon. They have a list of the week's activities posted there. And you can rent all kinds of equipment."

"Great," said Sam. "Do you think they have snowboards? I want to try snowboarding while I'm here."

"They probably have them. They have just about everything you could think of," said Mitch.

"Can we go right now?" I asked, pulling off my moose ears.

"Well, we have not finished unpacking yet," said Elizabeth. "But it would be nice to take a walk after our long drive."

We walked over to the lodge together. Really I did not walk. I ran!

I headed straight for the bulletin board. I wanted to see what activities were planned for the week. The two I liked best were going to be held the next Saturday. They were:

Valentine's Day Dance
Bring a friend and dance the night away
Winter Carnival
A fun-filled day of ski races, skating contests, a snow sculpture contest, and more!

"Cool!" I said. "I definitely want to go to the dance." (Valentine's Day is one of my favorite holidays.) "But first I will enter lots of contests. Saturday is going to be a very busy day."

"Hey, look," called Sam. He pointed to a sign at the rental desk. "They have them. They have the snowboards. I wonder if I can rent one right now."

"Maybe we can rent skis now, too," said Kristy.

"Oh, boy! Let's go skiing!" I cried.

Daddy checked at the rental desk. But we were too late. The desk was closing for the afternoon.

"Try us again first thing tomorrow," said the woman behind the desk.

24

"Sorry, kids. We will have to wait to go skiing," said Daddy.

"But we do not have to wait to have hot chocolate," said Nannie. "Look. They are serving some by the fire."

Yum. Hot chocolate. I headed for the table where it was being served.

"Ten cups of hot chocolate, please," I said to the waiter.

The waiter gave me a funny look.

"Oh, they are not all for me," I explained. "I have a very big family."

I pointed to my family. They were standing across the room. The man smiled. "Ten cups of hot chocolate coming right up," he said.

I could tell this was going to be a good vacation.

6

Snow Bunnies

First thing on Sunday morning, Daddy said, "Is everybody ready?"

"Ready!" we answered.

We had taken a vote to decide whether to eat at the lodge or in the house. The lodge won by a landslide.

We got a great big table all to ourselves. We ordered everything on the menu. There was bacon, eggs, pancakes, waffles, cereal, juice, coffee for the grown-ups, and hot chocolate for the kids.

"Okay," I said when we finished. "I am ready for skiing!"

My whole family was going. Well, almost my whole family. Sam was going to try snowboarding. And Nannie said she thought she was too old and Emily was too young to ski.

"We will be fine here at the lodge," she said.

It took forever to get onto the slopes. First we had to wait on line to rent our skis. Then we had to wait on line to get fitted. Then we had to wait on line to sign up for the right group. (Andrew and I were going to be in the snow bunny class.)

Finally we were heading for the ski lift with our class.

"This is going to be so great!" I said. "I am going to fly down the mountain."

"Me, too," said Andrew.

I thought about telling him not to get his hopes up too high. But he would find out soon enough that skiing is not so easy for a little kid like him.

Andrew and I had to wait on one more line to get on the ski lift. The next thing we knew we were being carried up the mountain. The snow bunnies' mountain was not very high. But the ride was still fun.

I could hardly wait to get to the top. I could hardly wait to start skiing.

The ski lift slowed and I stepped off. *Plompff.* I fell down and got a face full of snow. Boy, was I surprised. I quickly got up and brushed myself off.

"Are you okay, Karen?" asked Andrew. "What happened?"

"My skis got tangled up. Or something," I said.

My knees felt kind of wobbly. I looked back down the mountain. Somehow it looked higher than it did before.

"All right, class," called our instructor. "Gather round."

Our instructor's name was Toby. Toby talked to us about skiing for awhile. Then she said, "The best way to learn is by doing. We will not try skiing downhill right away.

I want you to start practicing right here where it is flat."

I could not even do that right. I tried once and fell down. *Plompff.* I tried again. *Plompff.* I tried again and again and again. *Plompff. Plompff. Plompff!*

While I was picking myself up and brushing myself off, the other kids started skiing down the hill. *All* the other kids. Including Andrew. He was flying down the slope like a pro.

"Would you like some help getting down the mountain?" asked Toby.

"No, thank you," I replied. "I am sure I can make it down myself."

I was not really sure at all. But I was too embarrassed to let anyone help me. Even my little brother was skiing down the slope by himself.

Finally I decided I was just too scared. I took off my skis and started to walk.

I was so, so humiliated.

7

Feeling Grumpy

I walked into the lodge and pushed my skis across the rental desk.

"Would you like the same pair tomorrow?" asked the woman at the desk with a smile.

"No way," I said. "I never, ever want to ski again."

I stomped away. I knew I should tell the woman I was sorry for sounding so mean. But I was too upset to say anything nice to anybody.

That included Nannie and Emily. I found

them reading books by the fire. (Really, Emily was looking at the pictures. She did not know how to read words yet.)

"How was skiing?" asked Nannie.

"Do not even ask me," I said. "But if you want to know the truth, I am never going skiing again."

"Why don't you tell me what happened," said Nannie.

"I do not want to talk about it," I said.

Then I sat down, took off my ski jacket, and told Nannie the whole story.

"I kept falling over and over again," I said. "I was down in the snow more than I was standing up!"

"You just need to practice," said Nannie calmly. "You are good at many things. I am sure you could learn to ski if you tried."

"I do not want to try anymore, Nannie," I said. Then I leaned in a little closer. I did not want the whole lodge to hear what I was going to say next. "I am too scared."

Just then the man next to us said, "Look at that little guy go."

I looked out the window in time to see Andrew skiing down the slope. I could not believe what a good skier he was. He was the youngest in the class. But he was the best. Everybody knew it.

"He is a terrific skier for his age," said the man's friend.

"He is a terrific skier for any age," said the man.

I covered my ears. I did not want to hear any more about Andrew and his terrific skiing.

I crossed my arms and started kicking the chair with my feet. Hearing about Andrew *goody two-skis* made me feel even worse than before.

"Karen," said Nannie. "Emily and I had a lot of fun looking around the lodge. There is so much going on. Why don't you take a walk and see for yourself."

I was not finished being grumpy yet. I kicked the chair a few more times. Then I decided it would be just as easy to be grumpy while I was walking around.

34

"Okay," I said. "I will see you later."

" 'Bye-bye," said Emily, waving.

You know what? The minute I stood up I felt a whole lot better.

8

The Lodge

I started in the video game room. I had played Pac-Man a lot over the summer. I liked that game. I found a quarter in my pocket and dropped it into the slot.

Ping ping. Ping ping ping.

"Go, Pac-Man, go!" I said. My Pac-Man had a big appetite. He was eating everything in his path. *Ping ping.* "Go, Pac-Man, go."

Soon he had cleared off the entire screen. A sign flashed, "You won! You won! You won!"

I might not be so good at skiing. But I was still good at Pac-Man. I played two more games. Then I decided to go to the library to look at magazines.

On the way I ran into Jessica. Jessica is Mitch's niece. She is nine. Jessica lives at Shadow Lake all year round. We had already said hi to each other at breakfast.

Jessica was standing by the snack machine. She did not look too happy.

"What is wrong?" I asked.

"I am mad at this machine. I put in two dimes and a nickel. The machine made a weird noise and spit out my dimes. Now I don't have pretzels. And I don't have another nickel."

"I have a nickel," I said. "Here. Try again."

I handed Jessica a nickel. She put the money into the machine. Then she pressed the pretzel button.

Guess what. *Two* bags of pretzels came out instead of one. We sat down together and had pretzels and hot chocolate.

"I saw your brother, Andrew, on the bunny slope before. He is a good skiier," said Jessica. "Why aren't you skiing, too?"

"I did not feel like it today," I said. (I did not tell Jessica that I would never feel like it again in my whole life.) "How about you?"

"I skied early in the morning. It is much less crowded then. And I am going ice skating later," said Jessica.

"Really? I like ice skating. I got a new pair of skates for Christmas," I said.

"Maybe I will see you at the pond then," said Jessica.

"Thanks for the pretzels," I said.

"Thanks for the nickel," said Jessica.

I was having a very good time at the lodge. A lot of people who remembered me from the summer said hi. A few kids even asked me if I wanted to go outside and play with them.

I said no thank you. I was in the mood to stay inside and read magazines at the library. But it was good to know there were outside things to do besides skiing.

9

Keegan

On Sunday night I dreamed I was ice skating in the Olympics. I did a triple twist jump backflip spin. The crowds went wild cheering for Karen Brewer, gold medal ice skater.

When I woke up on Monday morning, I was ready to skate. I put on my black leggings and my red sweater with snowflakes on it. Then I took out my new ice skates. Granny and Grandad had given them to me for Christmas. They were gigundoly beautiful.

Most of my family was already in the kitchen eating breakfast.

"Who wants to go skating with me?" I asked.

"Not me," said Sam. "I am going snowboarding."

"Sorry, Karen," said Daddy. "I promised myself I would ski as much as I could this vacation."

"Me, too," said Kristy. "We can always go skating in Stoneybrook. But we cannot ski there."

Elizabeth and David Michael said they were going skiing, too. (I did not even ask Andrew, the snow champ. I knew he would ski.)

"Where is Nannie?" I asked. "Maybe she will go skating with me."

"Emily has a cold this morning," said Elizabeth. "Nannie is going to stay here and take care of her."

Boo and bullfrogs. I was not allowed to go on the ice alone. But wait. I had seen a list of ice skating classes when I was at the lodge. Of course I was already a gold medal skater. But I could still join a class. Maybe the teacher would ask me to demonstrate one of my excellent skating routines. Or I could skate around by myself while the class was going on. I just wanted to get out on the ice.

I grabbed my things and hurried over to the lodge. I checked the bulletin board. There was a big sign that said: Skating canceled due to warm weather.

Warm weather in February? Just my luck. Now what? I was tired of playing Pac-Man. I had read all my favorite magazines at the library. I started wandering around the lodge. It was pretty empty. Except for the rental desk. Everyone was renting skis.

"See you later, Dad," said a boy. He waved good-bye to a man walking out with skis under his arm. I remembered the boy from the day before. He was in the snow-bunny class. I watched him go into the video game room.

The boy was standing in front of Turtle

Terror. I knew that game was more fun to play with two people. I went into the game room.

"Hi," I said. "Want to play?"

"Sure," said the boy.

We played two games. We each won one.

"My name is Karen," I said. "What is yours?"

"My name is Keegan," said the boy.

I asked Keegan why he was not skiing. He shrugged his shoulders and said, "No big reason. I just do not like it that much. My parents are *big* skiers. But not me."

"I do not like skiing so much either," I replied. "Hey, do you want to check out the snack machine? Yesterday it was giving out two bags of pretzels for twenty-five cents."

"Sure. Let's go," said Keegan.

I put in a dime. Keegan put in a dime and a nickel.

"Abracadabra!" I said. I pushed the pretzel button. Only one bag came out. (I did not mind. I would have felt bad getting too many free bags of pretzels.)

We shared the pretzels. Then we decided to play a game of Monopoly. We ended up spending the whole morning together. It was fun.

I decided I liked Keegan.

Fun at Shadow Lake

Keegan was already at the lodge when I got there Tuesday morning. He was looking at the bulletin board.

"Hi, Keegan," I said. "What are you going to do today?"

"Right now I am trying to decide what to do in the winter carnival," he replied. "I cannot decide whether to enter the snow sculpture contest or the ice skating contest."

"Those are the contests I like, too," I said.

"Let's do both," said Keegan.

"All right!" I replied. "We better start practicing."

We agreed to start with our snow sculpture. I told Nannie that Keegan and I were going outside. (Emily's cold was a little bit better. So Nannie and Emily were going to be hanging around at the lodge.)

"Please stay in front where I can watch you," said Nannie.

"We will make a beautiful sculpture for you and Emily to look at," I said.

Do you know what? We did. We built a great, big, huge, enormous snow castle.

"Maybe we could make colored flags. We could put them all over the castle on the day of the contest," I said.

"Okay," said Keegan. "And I think we should have a snow horse standing outside our castle. In case someone wants to ride off into the forest."

Our snow horse came out looking more like a camel. But that was okay. We had plenty of time to practice getting it right.

"Brrr. I'm cold!" I said.

"Me, too," said Keegan.

"Let's go inside. We can look at the bulletin board again," I said. "If it is this cold out, I bet there will be an ice skating class."

There *was* an ice skating class. And it was not even filled up yet. (That is because practically everyone else was skiing.)

We drank some hot chocolate to warm us up. We already had our skates with us. So we were ready to head out to Beaver Pond. (Shadow Lake is too big to get frozen over completely. Beaver Pond does not take as long to freeze because it is smaller.)

The pond was just down the road from the lodge. The green flags were up. (That meant the ice was safe for skating.) The class was just starting.

Maybe I was the worst skier. But I was definitely not the worst skater. In fact, Keegan and I were the best on the ice. I thought about doing my triple twist jump backflip spin. But I did not want to be a show-off. Plus I had only done it once in my dream. So I probably needed some practice.

When the class was over, we went back to the lodge to meet our families.

"See you tomorrow!" I called to Keegan.

" 'Bye, Karen," Keegan replied.

The day had been so much fun. Nothing could ruin it. Not even finding out that Andrew's snow bunny class was going to race in the winter carnival. Not even listening to *everyone* say that Andrew was sure to win.

So what? Skiing was not the only way to have a good time at Shadow Lake. Now I was having fun, too.

11

Family Day Morning

Everyone was up bright and early on Wednesday morning.

"How are you feeling, Emily?" asked Elizabeth.

"All better!" Emily replied. She threw her arms up in the air to show everyone how good she felt.

"That is excellent news," said Daddy. "Since we are on vacation and everyone is feeling good, I now declare this day Family Day!"

"Hooray!" I cried. Then I added, "What is Family Day?"

I knew about all kinds of holidays. But I had never heard of a Family Day before.

Daddy explained, "It is a day we will spend doing activities together as a family."

"We can start off with a picnic," said Elizabeth. "It will be an indoor breakfast picnic. We can spread out our blanket in front of the fireplace."

We all thought this was a gigundoly wonderful idea.

"Everyone has to pitch in," said Daddy.

"That means we need to get organized," said Nannie. "Here are your assignments."

Nannie assigned one job, plus clean-up duty, to each person.

Kristy was going to make the toast. David Michael was going to set out plates and cups and napkins on a table. Sam was going to squeeze oranges for juice.

"Karen, you are in charge of the eggs," said Nannie. "It is your job to break them open and beat them."

"Oh, that is mean!" I said. Everyone laughed.

I even got to have an assistant. It was Emily's job to throw away the shells after I broke open the eggs. We had great fun working together.

Our breakfast was a Family Day feast! We were nice and cozy in front of our crackling fire.

Bzzz Bzzz Bzzz.

"What are you doing, Karen?" asked Charlie.

"I am buzzing like a bee. A real picnic always has bees," I replied. "And ants, too. There goes one now!"

I started brushing make-believe ants off our blanket. Emily thought this was hysterical.

"Clean-up time!" called Daddy.

When everything was put away, it was time for our next Family Day activity. We bundled up and went out into the snow. First we went snowmobiling. I love going really fast!

Then Sam gave us a snowboarding show. The snowboard was bright purple. It looked like a giant skateboard with a strap across it.

"Snowboarding is really easy. I will demonstrate," said Sam. "You will see that it is a cross between skateboarding, surfing, and skiing."

As soon as I heard the word skiing I knew snowboarding was not for me. But I had fun watching.

When Sam finished his show, we decided to build a snow family in honor of the day. We were working really hard. People passing by stopped to watch as our snow family grew. When we finished, we had a family of ten, just like ours.

"I am so glad I brought my camera," said

Elizabeth. "Gather round, everyone."

We asked a passerby to please take our picture.

"Smile!" said the woman.

She did not even have to say it. We were so proud of our snow family. Our smiles were already a mile wide.

Family Day Afternoon

The morning flew by. It was lunchtime before we knew it.

"Who wants to eat at the lodge?" asked Daddy.

"I do! I do!" I said.

Everyone else had the same answer. The ten of us marched into the dining room. I waved as I passed Keegan and his parents. I love making a grand entrance.

There were no big tables left. So we had to split up.

"Can we sit at our own kids' table?" I added.

"I don't see why not," said Daddy.

This is how we sat: Daddy, Elizabeth, Nannie, Sam, and Charlie were at one table. Andrew, David Michael, Kristy, Emily, and I were at another. (Kristy was in charge of watching Emily. She is an excellent babysitter.)

Sitting at our table without any grownups made me feel like a real and true Lovely Lady. I sat up tall in my chair. I held my pinky up in the air as I lifted my napkin and placed it in my lap.

My manners were perfect all the way through lunch. I only stopped one time to blow bubbles in my soup. *Blub blub blub.* (Andrew started it. Not me.)

After lunch we took a vote and decided to go ice skating. Yippee!

"I am going to be in the ice skating contest with Keegan next Saturday," I told everyone as we were walking to the pond.

"That sounds great," said Kristy.

"We skate really well together," I said.

It is nice to feel that you are good at something. I know I am good at skating. I could hardly wait to get on the ice.

"I am going to be in the ski race," said Andrew. "But I do not think I will win. I am the youngest snow bunny."

"Being the youngest will not stop you from winning," said Sam. "I have seen you ski. You are the best in your class."

I did not want to think about skiing anymore. It is no fun thinking about something you are not so good at. Unless you plan to get better. And I was not going to get better at skiing because I was not going to try it ever again.

We reached the pond. Nannie and Emily waved to us from the side. The rest of us skated around in pairs. I skated with Kristy. We glided and twirled.

"Wow, Karen. You really are a good skater," said Kristy.

"Thank you," I replied.

We skated for a long time. Then we went

home and made dinner. We had spaghetti, salad, and rolls. For dessert, we toasted marshmallows in the fire.

"Here's to our family!" said Daddy. "It has been a wonderful day."

We held up our marshmallows and tapped them together.

"To our family!" we said.

13

Practicing

I met Keegan at the lodge early Thursday morning.

"Do you want to go to the pond first?" I asked. "I saw the skating teacher before. She said she would keep an eye on us."

(There always had to be a grown-up watching us on the ice. That was Daddy's rule.)

"Sure. Let's go," said Keegan.

We took turns showing each other which moves we thought looked the best. Then we picked our favorites and tried to do them together. I called out the moves.

"Forward," I said. "Now circle. Forward. Now figure eight."

"That looks terrific, kids," said our teacher. "What you are doing is called pair skating. You are working as a real team. I think it would look nice to hold hands when you skate forward or in a circle. Then take turns skating apart for the figure eights."

We tried our routine again holding hands. This time Keegan called out the moves.

"Forward," he said. "Circle. Forward. Figure eight."

At first we had a little trouble circling together. We practiced all morning until we got it right.

"We can meet outside later to work on our snow sculpture," said Keegan. "I have to meet my mom and dad for lunch now."

On the way back to the lodge, we saw Andrew skiing down the slope.

"Your little brother really is a good skier," said Keegan.

"He is going to win the race on Saturday. I just know it," I replied.

"Maybe we will win something, too," Keegan said. "See you later."

I ate at the house with Nannie and Emily. Sam was busy snowboarding. Everyone else was skiing.

When we finished lunch, we walked back to the lodge together. Keegan was waiting for me inside.

"I am ready," I said.

We found a place where Nannie could watch us.

"I do not think we should worry about the castle now," said Keegan. "We need to practice making our snow horse."

"You are right," I said. "It would be hard to explain why there was a camel guarding our castle."

While we were working, we tried to check out the competition. We looked at the other people trying out their sculptures.

We saw an igloo, a car, and some sculptures that were just pretty shapes. But I did not think anything looked as good as our castle.

We tried our best to make a horse. We ended up with a dog instead.

"Um, dog, do you think you could turn into a horse?" I asked.

"Woof! Woof!" barked Keegan. "He says he likes being a dog."

Nannie was waving for us to come inside. I quickly made a snow bone and gave it to our snow dog. Then I made a plan with Keegan to meet in the morning for more practicing.

The next day, our skating routine went perfectly. Our castle looked great. But we still could not get the horse right. We kept making the same dog. "Maybe we should just make the castle," I said.

"I think you are right," said Keegan. "The carnival starts at ten o'clock tomorrow. Do you want to meet inside the lodge at nine?"

"I will be there," I replied.

There were butterflies in my stomach. I was a little nervous about the carnival. But that was not the only thing I was nervous about. I was thinking about the Valentine's Day dance, too. It would be held the next night.

I was wondering if I would get to dance with Keegan. I really, really hoped I would.

The Accident

I was up early the next morning. It was Saturday, the day of the winter carnival.

I hurried to get dressed. Then I gathered up the flags I had made for our castle. They were triangles of colored paper glued onto matching straws. I wrapped the flags in plastic so they would not get wet.

"Happy winter carnival day!" I said, marching into the kitchen.

"Good morning," said Nannie. "I know that you and Andrew need to get to the lodge early. I will take you over. The rest of the family can meet us later."

"I am going over early, too," said Sam. "I promised Andrew I would take him up the slope a few times before the contest."

We ate our breakfast. Then Nannie, Sam, Andrew, and I walked over to the lodge.

"I bet you will win the contest," I said to Andrew on the way.

"The teacher said I should not worry about winning," Andrew replied. "She said I should just do my best."

"If you do your best, you will win," I said. "*Everyone* says you are the best skier in the group."

I did not say it so nicely. That is because I wished I were the one entering an important ski contest. I wished I were the one everyone expected to win.

When we reached the lodge, Sam and Andrew waved good-bye and headed for the slopes. Keegan was outside waiting for me.

"Hi, Keegan!" I said. "I am ready for the carnival."

"Have a good time, you two," said Nannie. "I will be inside the lodge if you need me."

There was a big area marked off for the snow sculpture contest. Keegan and I walked around looking for the best spot for our castle.

We were still looking when we noticed people pointing toward one of the ski slopes. There was a big commotion at the top of the slope.

"What happened?" I asked.

"There was an accident," said a woman who had just come back from skiing. "A little boy fell. It looked like he got hurt."

"And he was such a good skier, too," said the woman's friend.

"That could be Andrew!" I said to Keegan.

"Yes," said the woman. "That was the boy's name. I heard someone say it."

"Oh, no!" I cried. "Andrew was in an accident!"

I looked toward the lodge. Nannie was not in her usual spot. I did not see anyone from my family at all.

"I want to go up there. Sam and Andrew might need me," I said to Keegan.

"Come on," Keegan replied. "We will grab some skis and go up the lift. That will be the fastest way."

We quickly got skis. We put them on, then rode the lift up the mountain.

When we reached the top, Toby was kneeling next to Andrew. I hurried over to my little brother.

"It is okay, Andrew," I said. "I am here. I will not leave you alone for one second."

Andrew tried to smile. He was being very brave.

"Sam went to get the Ski Patrol," said Toby. "They will bring a snowmobile and a sled to pull Andrew down the mountain."

All we could do was wait for Sam and

the Ski Patrol to come back. It was cold and windy on the mountain. I held Andrew's hand and did not let go. We waited and waited. It felt like forever. Finally they came. We all helped Andrew onto the snowmobile.

"You will be okay, Andrew," I said. "I promise."

Then I watched them disappear down the mountain.

15

Skiing

"I hope Andrew will be okay," I said to Keegan. "He looked scared."

"You helped him a lot," Keegan replied. "It is good we came up here."

"Up here?" I repeated.

Suddenly I realized where I was. I was way up on a ski slope. All I had been thinking about for the past half hour was Andrew. Now I had time to think about me. How was I going to get down the mountain? I was terrified of skiing.

I thought about taking my skis off and walking down. But I did not want to do that. It would be too humiliating.

"Are you ready to ski down the mountain?" asked Keegan.

I had told Keegan I did not like skiing. But I had not told him I was scared of it. And I did not feel like telling him now.

"I am ready," I replied. "Just remember I have not done much skiing. I need to go really, really slowly."

"No problem," said Keegan. "I will help you. Look, if you ski at an angle like this, you will go slower."

Keegan went down a little way to show me what he meant. He was going back and forth across the slope, instead of straight down. I could see he was not going very fast.

"If you want to go even slower or stop completely, you do something called the 'snowplow,' " said Keegan. "Just put your knees together like this."

When he put his knees together a certain way, the front of his skis came together, too, in a point. There was no way to go too fast when the skis were pointing at each other.

Keegan came back up and stood next to me. I took a deep breath. Then slowly, very slowly, we skied down the mountain together.

A couple of times I felt so scared I wanted to sit down in the snow. But I did not do it. Instead I put my knees together the way Keegan showed me. That made me go slowly enough so I was not scared anymore.

Little by little we skied down the slope. Little by little we came closer to the bottom. Little by little we made it!

What a relief. I still did not like skiing. But at least I was not so scared of it anymore. Being scared was the worst part.

We took off our skis. Then I said to Keegan, "We have to hurry to the lodge. We have to find out how Andrew is."

16

The First Contest

I raced into the lodge to find my family.

"Here comes Karen!" called David Michael.

I was out of breath by the time I reached them. They were waiting outside the video game room. That is where the telephones were. Only Daddy, Sam, and Andrew were missing.

"Where did they take Andrew? How is he?" I asked.

"They took him to the hospital emergency room," said Elizabeth. "We have not heard how he is yet. We are waiting for Daddy to call us."

At that very minute the phone rang. Elizabeth answered it. She listened for awhile and nodded her head. Then she said into the phone, "Yes, I will tell them."

"Is Andrew going to be all right?" I asked.

"Andrew is going to be fine," Elizabeth replied. "But he did hurt himself. He twisted his knee badly. He will not be able to walk for awhile. And of course skiing is out of the question."

Poor Andrew. I felt really bad that he was hurt. I felt worse that he could not ski. I knew the contest was important to him. He was excited about being in it. I felt bad that I had been grouchy before, too. That was not fair. It was not Andrew's fault that he was a good skier and I was not.

There was a lot to think about. But I did not get to think very long. An announcement was being made over the loudspeaker in the lodge.

"Anyone entering the ice skating contest please go to Beaver Pond now."

"That is us," said Keegan. "We have to go."

Keegan grabbed my hand. We ran to the pond together.

We put on our skates, laced them up, and waited for our turn on the ice. It was not long before our names were announced.

"Our next partners on ice are Karen Brewer and Keegan Ross."

I was so excited. The first thing I did was trip on my way to the pond. Luckily Keegan caught me. I knew I was still a little shaky from all the excitement. Andrew had been in an accident. I had skied down a mountain. Now I was going to be in an ice skating contest. Concentrate, Karen, concentrate, I said to myself.

Keegan looked at me and smiled. I smiled back.

"We are on," he said.

We stepped out onto the ice. The minute

I started to skate, everything else went out of my mind. The air was cold, the ice was smooth. I felt so happy.

We knew our routine by heart. Forward. Circle. Forward. Figure eight.

I could feel everyone's eyes on Keegan and me. When we finished I heard lots of clapping. A few voices were yelling, "Yeah, Karen! Yeah, Keegan!" Our families were cheering for us. I turned and took a bow.

We did not win the contest. But I did not mind. I had fun. And I knew I had skated well.

There was one more thing I knew. I could skate — and now I could ski if I wanted to.

17

The Second Contest

When we got back to the lodge, Daddy, Sam, and Andrew were there. Andrew had a brace on his leg. And he was trying to use crutches.

"How do you feel?" I asked him.

"I guess I feel okay. My leg does not hurt too much," Andrew replied. "But I am so mad I missed my race."

Andrew looked as if he were going to cry. I wanted to do something to make him feel better.

"I know what!" I said. "You could help Keegan and me with our snow sculpture. You can be in the contest with us." I looked at Keegan.

"That is a great idea," Keegan said.

Andrew's face lit up.

"Thanks, Karen. Thanks, Keegan," he said.

The contest began after lunch. We found a spot where our families could watch us from inside the lodge.

"You have half an hour to build your snow sculpture," said one of the judges. "When you hear the whistle, you may begin."

The judge blew the whistle and we got to work. Andrew could not get around very well. I needed to think of a job he could do without walking much.

"Hey, Andrew," I said. "You can be our director. Just like in the movies."

Andrew liked that idea. I think he liked it a little too much.

"Make that tower higher," said Andrew.

I made the tower higher.

"No. That is too high," said Andrew. "Make it this high."

He waved his crutch in the air to show me how high to make the tower.

I made it lower. Then even lower. Higher. Lower.

"Hey, Andrew, why don't you put these flags on the castle?" said Keegan.

"Yes, the flags are very important," I said.

That was the perfect job for Andrew. He did not have to walk much. And Keegan and I could finish building the castle.

We did our best. When we finished it was a little lopsided. And it was smaller than we had planned.

I looked at the other sculptures. Some of them were good. Really good. Next to them, our castle did not look all that great. The best thing about it was the colored flags on top.

The judge blew the whistle.

"It is time to stop working," she said. "Please stand by your sculpture. The judges will come around to each of you."

There were three judges. When they got to us, one of them said to Andrew, "I am sorry about your accident. I saw you skiing yesterday. You are very good."

"Thank you," Andrew replied.

"What was your job here today?" asked the judge.

"I was the director! And I put on the flags, too," said Andrew proudly.

"Oh, I see," the judge replied. He jotted something down in his notebook.

Finally it was time to announce the winners. A sculpture of a snow angel won. I could see why. She was a very beautiful angel. She had a gold halo and everything.

Our castle got an honorable mention. I had the feeling they gave it to us because of Andrew. I think they wanted him to win something because they felt bad about his accident.

It was the second contest we did not win. But we had fun being in it. And that was the most important thing.

18

The Phone Call

The carnival lasted until late afternoon. Then we ate dinner at the lodge. Then it was time to go home to get ready for the Valentine's Day dance. Saturday had been a very exciting day!

I had lost track of Keegan by dinnertime. He probably went home with his parents to eat. He had not said anything to me about going to the dance. So I was not even sure he would be there. Boo.

I decided to have a good time anyway. Even if I did not get to dance with Keegan.

"What are you going to wear tonight?" I asked Kristy.

We were standing in front of the closet deciding what to put on.

"It is not a fancy party. So I am going to wear my jeans and a sweatshirt," Kristy replied. (I was not surprised. Kristy always wears jeans and a sweatshirt.)

"Then I will, too," I replied.

I put on my dark blue jeans and my light blue sweatshirt.

"That was easy," I said to Kristy. "I am all ready."

The phone was ringing in the other room. Nannie answered it. Then she called, "Karen, it is for you. It is Keegan."

Hmm. I wonder what he wants to tell me, I thought.

"Hi, Keegan," I said.

Guess what. Keegan did not have something to tell me. He had something to ask me. He called to ask me to be his date at the Valentine's Day dance.

"Your *date*?" I said. "Of course I will be your date."

We planned to meet at the lodge at seven-thirty. I could hardly believe it! I was going to be Keegan's date at the Valentine's Day dance.

I looked down at my jeans and sweatshirt. This was not a good outfit for an important date. I hurried back to the room to change my clothes.

Red. I needed to wear red for Valentine's Day. I pulled out my red corduroy jumper. Then I found a red cotton turtleneck, and red tights.

I put everything on and looked in the mirror. Just then, Daddy passed by.

"Karen, you look beautiful," said Daddy.

"Thank you," I replied. I hoped Keegan would think so, too.

The Dance

"Hi, Karen!" called Keegan. "Hey, you are all dressed in red. You look like a red lollipop."

Hmm. I wondered if that was Keegan's way of saying I looked beautiful. I decided that it was.

"Thank you," I replied.

"Want to go in and get some punch?" asked Keegan.

I had been hoping he would ask me to dance right away. I could see I was going to have to wait. Keegan and I walked together to the main room at the lodge. That is where the dance was being held.

"Can I go in with you?" asked Andrew.

Uh-oh. Somehow Andrew had caught up with us even on his crutches. It was okay for him to make the sculpture with us. But I did not want him tagging along on my date. I did not have much choice, though.

"Sure," said Keegan. "Come on."

The decorations in the main room were very beautiful. Everywhere you looked were red hearts, red balloons, and red crepe paper streamers.

There were pitchers of punch and stacks of cups on a table. And there were big bowls filled with jelly beans and chocolate kisses.

"Can I have some punch?" asked Andrew.

I poured some punch into a cup for him. He put both crutches in one hand. He held the cup with the other.

"I would like jelly beans, too," said Andrew.

I filled another cup with jelly beans.

"Karen, will you hold my crutches?" asked Andrew.

I took the crutches from him. And Andrew turned to Keegan. "Want to hear about my accident?" he said.

Something was not right. I was holding Andrew's crutches. He was drinking punch, eating candy, and talking to Keegan. Suddenly Elizabeth appeared. She took the crutches from me.

"Come on, Andrew," she said. "We have our own table over there."

She led Andrew to a table where Daddy, Nannie, and Emily were sitting. Thank you, Elizabeth!

Then it was just Keegan and me. We were having a real date. For a while we talked to Jessica and some other kids we had met. Then we stood around, drinking punch and eating candy.

I kept hoping Keegan would ask me to dance. Then I thought, maybe I should ask *him*. Before I had a chance, Keegan turned to me and said, "Do you want to dance, Karen?"

I wanted to jump up and down, wave my arms, and shout yippee! But I did not. I just said, "Sure, I would love to dance."

We walked to the center of the dance floor. Colored lights were flashing. The band was playing a great song. And I was dancing with my date. I felt very happy and very grown-up.

We stayed on the dance floor a long time. We were still there when the band stopped playing.

"Thank you for coming tonight, everyone," said the bandleader. "And happy Valentine's Day!"

The Valentine's Day dance was over. My week at Shadow Lake was almost over, too. The next day we would arrive back to Stoneybrook.

My family walked out of the lodge with Keegan's family. Our houses were in different directions. So it was time to say good-bye.

"See you next year!" said Keegan.

"See you next year!" I replied.

Then we waved good-bye and headed home with our families.

Good-bye, Shadow Lake

On Sunday morning after breakfast, Mitch stopped in to say good-bye. We thanked him again for making the cabin so cozy for our vacation.

"I am always glad to help," Mitch replied.

When Mitch left, I started to pack my suitcase. I tried to do it myself. But somehow I could not get everything to fit the way it had before.

"I do not understand," I said to Kristy.

"I did not buy anything while I was here."

Kristy took one look at my jumble of things and shook her head.

"I think you need my mom," she said.

I found Elizabeth. She helped me fold and roll my things. It was magic! Suddenly everything fit into my suitcase just like before.

We were not ready to go yet. So I hurried outside. I wanted to do as many vacation things as I could before we left.

First I threw myself down in the snow and made a snow angel. Then I made snowballs. I ran inside and asked if anyone wanted to have a snowball fight.

"I am not finished packing," said David Michael.

"I do not want to get all wet," said Kristy.

No one wanted to come outside to play. So I decided to build a snowman instead. The snowman was half finished when Daddy came outside.

"It is time to get your bags, Karen," he said. "I would like to start packing the van."

"Can I get them in a minute?" I asked. "I want to finish my snowman."

"I am sorry but you have to stop now. You can build another snowman when we get home. There will be snow in Stoneybrook, too," said Daddy. "I promise."

I had wanted to build my snowman with Shadow Lake snow. But building a snowman in Stoneybrook would be fun, too. I could build it with Hannie and Nancy. While we were building it, I would tell them about my vacation. I wanted to tell them about Keegan. I wanted to tell them about Andrew's accident. And I wanted to tell them how I skied down the mountain!

Suddenly I could hardly wait to get home. I wanted to see my friends. I wanted to see Mommy and Seth. I ran inside and got my bags.

In no time we were in our seats and ready to go.

"Buckle up, everyone," said Daddy.

We buckled our seat belts. Then Daddy pulled the van out of the driveway and headed down the road. Elizabeth followed behind in the car.

When I turned around, Shadow Lake was growing smaller and smaller in the distance. I waved and said, "Good-bye, Shadow Lake. Thank you for a wonderful vacation."

About the Author

ANN M. MARTIN lives in New York City and loves animals, especially cats. She has two cats of her own, Mouse and Rosie.

Other books by Ann M. Martin that you might enjoy are *Stage Fright; Me and Katie (the Pest);* and the books in *The Baby-sitters Club* series.

Ann likes ice cream and *I Love Lucy*. And she has her own little sister, whose name is Jane.

Little Sister

Don't miss #59
KAREN'S LEPRECHAUN

When we were all gathered around him, Mr. O'Casey whispered, "I am a leprechaun. A leprechaun is a real and true fairy."

Andrew's eyes opened wide and his mouth dropped open. "Is that like the tooth fairy?" he asked.

"Why, yes, I suppose it is," said Mr. O'Casey.

He told us that he came from a long line of leprechauns who fixed the shoes of dancing fairies.

"Leprechauns keep pots of gold hidden away in a special place. To find the gold, you have to go all the way to the end of a rainbow," he whispered.

Then he asked us to close our eyes and count to ten. When we opened them again, he was gone!

LITTLE APPLE®

BABY-SITTERS

Little Sister™

by Ann M. Martin, author of *The Baby-sitters Club*®

☐ MQ44300-3 #1	Karen's Witch	$2.95
☐ MQ44259-7 #2	Karen's Roller Skates	$2.95
☐ MQ44299-7 #3	Karen's Worst Day	$2.95
☐ MQ44264-3 #4	Karen's Kittycat Club	$2.95
☐ MQ44258-9 #5	Karen's School Picture	$2.95
☐ MQ44298-8 #6	Karen's Little Sister	$2.95
☐ MQ44257-0 #7	Karen's Birthday	$2.95
☐ MQ42670-2 #8	Karen's Haircut	$2.95
☐ MQ43652-X #9	Karen's Sleepover	$2.95
☐ MQ43651-1 #10	Karen's Grandmothers	$2.95
☐ MQ43650-3 #11	Karen's Prize	$2.95
☐ MQ43649-X #12	Karen's Ghost	$2.95
☐ MQ43648-1 #13	Karen's Surprise	$2.75
☐ MQ43646-5 #14	Karen's New Year	$2.75
☐ MQ43645-7 #15	Karen's in Love	$2.75
☐ MQ43644-9 #16	Karen's Goldfish	$2.75
☐ MQ43643-0 #17	Karen's Brothers	$2.75
☐ MQ43642-2 #18	Karen's Home-Run	$2.75
☐ MQ43641-4 #19	Karen's Good-Bye	$2.95
☐ MQ44823-4 #20	Karen's Carnival	$2.75
☐ MQ44824-2 #21	Karen's New Teacher	$2.95
☐ MQ44833-1 #22	Karen's Little Witch	$2.95
☐ MQ44832-3 #23	Karen's Doll	$2.95
☐ MQ44859-5 #24	Karen's School Trip	$2.95
☐ MQ44831-5 #25	Karen's Pen Pal	$2.95
☐ MQ44830-7 #26	Karen's Ducklings	$2.75
☐ MQ44829-3 #27	Karen's Big Joke	$2.95
☐ MQ44828-5 #28	Karen's Tea Party	$2.95

More Titles... ➡

Available wherever you buy books, or use this order form.

THE BABY-SITTERS Club®

Claudia Kristy Mallory Stacey Dawn Mary Anne Jessi

Wow! It's really them—
the new Baby-sitters Club dolls!

Your favorite Baby-sitters Club characters have come to life in these
beautiful collector dolls. Each doll wears her own unique clothes and jewelry.
They look just like the girls you have imagined! The dolls also come with their own
individual stories in special edition booklets that you'll find nowhere else.

Look for the new Baby-sitters Club collection...
coming soon to a store near you!

Kenner